FLUFFY
AND THE FIREFIGHTERS

For Tommy, Jessica, and Nicholas Donato
— K.M.

To Matthew and Ross
— M.S.

The author would like to offer many thanks to all the
firefighters of Ladder Company 7 and Engine Company 16
of the New York City Fire Department, especially
Tommy Donato and Mike Boccia for their time and for their
excellent suggestions, which found their way into this story.

Text copyright © 1999 by Kate McMullan.
Illustrations copyright © 1999 Mavis Smith.

All rights reserved. Published by Scholastic Inc.
SCHOLASTIC, CARTWHEEL BOOKS, FLUFFY THE CLASSROOM GUINEA PIG,
and associated logos are trademarks and/or registered trademarks of Scholastic Inc.
Lexile is a registered trademark of MetaMetrics, Inc.

Library of Congress Cataloging-in-Publication Data is available.

ISBN-13: 978-0-439-12917-6
ISBN-10: 0-439-12917-6

11 10 9 8 7 6   09 10 11 12

Printed in the U.S.A. 23 • This edition first printing, July 2008

FLUFFY
AND THE FIREFIGHTERS

GROWING READER
LEVEL 3
700-1500 WORDS

by Kate McMullan
Illustrated by Mavis Smith

Cartwheel
·B·O·O·K·S·®

SCHOLASTIC INC.
New York Toronto London Auckland Sydney
Mexico City New Delhi Hong Kong Buenos Aires

Save the Pig!

Firefighter Tom and Firefighter Mike
came to Ms. Day's classroom.

"Hello, firefighters!" said all the kids.
Fluffy did not say anything.
He was having his morning nap.

"Hi, kids," said Firefighter Tom.
"We are here to tell you about our job.
Our uniforms help to protect us
when we fight fires. We wear turnout coats
and high rubber boots," Tom told the class.
Mike put on his turnout coat.
He stepped into his high rubber boots.
Fluffy turned over in his sleep.

"We wear thick gloves, too," said Tom.

Mike pulled on his thick gloves.

"We wear helmets to protect our heads,"
said Tom.

Mike put on his helmet.

"His helmet has a flashlight on it,"
Emma whispered to Wade.

"That helps him see in the dark."

Fluffy did not see anything.

He was in dreamland.

"Breathing too much smoke
makes people sick," said Firefighter Tom.
"So firefighters breathe air from
tanks on their backs."
Firefighter Mike put on his air tank.

He put a big mask over his face.
A hose connected the mask to the tank.
"Now Mike can breathe air
from the air tank," said Tom.
"Now he is ready to fight a fire."
"Hooray for firefighters!" said Maxwell.
Everyone clapped and cheered.

The cheering woke Fluffy.

He opened his eyes.

He saw Firefighter Mike.

Help! thought Fluffy.

A space monster has landed!

Call the police! Call the Marines!

Somebody save the pig!

Fluffy ran around his cage.
He squeaked and squeaked.
"I think Fluffy is scared of Mike,"
said Jasmine.
"Firefighters can look scary
when they are dressed to fight fires,"
Tom told the class.
"But firefighters are your friends."

Help! Help! thought Fluffy.
Mars invader!
Somebody save the pig!
Fluffy dove under his food dish.
"Fluffy is hiding from Mike,"
said Maxwell.

"If a firefighter comes to help you,"
said Tom, "do not go under your bed
or into a closet. Never ever hide
from a firefighter."

Firefighter? thought Fluffy.

He peeked out from under his food bowl.

Did someone say *firefighter*?

Firefighter Mike took off his mask.

"Hello, Fluffy," he said.

"Don't be scared of me."

Me? Scared? thought Fluffy.

Ha! You must be joking!

Fluffy's Wild Ride

"Our fire engine is parked outside,"
Tom told Ms. Day's class.
"Come and see it."
Everyone went outside.
Wade brought Fluffy, too.

"Firefighter Carolina drives the fire engine," said Tom. "We call her the *chauffeur*."
"Hi, kids," said Carolina. She waved.
All the kids waved back.
Fluffy waved, too.

"A fire engine is also called a pumper,"
said Mike. "It pumps water
from a fire hydrant through hoses."
Very cool, thought Fluffy.
I bet I could drive this fire engine.
I bet I could be a firefighter.

Firefighters Tom and Mike let the kids
sit in the cab of the fire engine.
Wade was last in line.
"Hot dog!" said Wade
when his turn finally came.

He climbed into the cab.
He put Fluffy down on the seat.
Wade looked at all the dials.
He pretended to steer the engine.

Then Wade climbed out of the cab.
He ran to get in line to hold a fire hose.
He forgot about Fluffy.

Fluffy was alone in the cab
of the fire engine.
All right! thought Fluffy.
I am a firefighter now!

Firefighter Fluffy
drove the fire engine fast.
He made the siren wail: *Whoop! Whoop!*
He honked the horn: *Beeeeeep! Beeeeeep!*
All the cars got out of the way.
Fluffy pulled up to the curb.
A store was on fire!

Fluffy connected a hose to a fire hydrant.

He aimed the hose at the fire.

Water shot from the nozzle: *Whoooosh!*

In no time, he put the fire out.

Fluffy! cried the guinea pigs.

You are our hero!

Nothing to it, said Fluffy.

Suddenly, Fluffy felt the fire
engine lurch. Firefighter Carolina
had jumped into the driver's seat.
She drove away from the school.
She zoomed around a corner.
Wow! thought Fluffy. **This is fast!**
Fluffy felt his breakfast gurgling
in his tummy.
He was not sure he liked going so fast.

Firefighter Carolina put on the siren.

WHOOP! WHOOP! WHOOP!

Yikes! thought Fluffy.

Carolina honked the horn.

BEEEEEEP! BEEEEEEP!

Jeepers! thought Fluffy.

He was not sure he liked so much noise.

The engine pulled up to a fire.
Fluffy felt the heat from the flames.
He was not sure he liked being so hot.
Fluffy was not sure he wanted to be
a firefighter after all.

A ladder truck pulled up next to the engine.
The firefighters began fighting the fire.
They worked as a team.
Some firefighters climbed tall ladders.
Some cut a hole in the roof
to let out the smoke.

Some ran into the building
to search for people
who might be trapped inside.
Some held hoses from up high in a bucket.
They fought the fire for a long time.

Fluffy watched from the fire engine.

He saw that the firefighters were very brave.

He saw how the firefighters
worked together as a team.

Now he wished he could be part
of a firefighting team.

Firefighters are real heroes,
thought Fluffy.

But how can a pig fight fires?

Firefighter Fluffy

At last Firefighters Tom, Mike, and Carolina
came back to the fire engine.
They put away their equipment.
Then they got into the cab.

Their faces were hot
and smudged with smoke.
Fluffy thought they looked tired.
But he thought they looked happy, too.
After all, they had put out a fire.
And they had saved people's lives.

"Well, look who's here," said Firefighter Tom.
He picked up Fluffy.

"Hi, Fluffy," said Mike.

"Fluffy," said Carolina, "are you trying to tell
us that you want to be a firefighter?"

You got that right, said Fluffy.

But how can I be a firefighter?

Carolina drove back to the firehouse.
Tom carried Fluffy inside.
He called Ms. Day.
He told her where he had found
Firefighter Fluffy.

"Firefighter Fluffy!" Ms. Day laughed.
"I will tell my students about that.
May I bring them to the firehouse
this afternoon to pick up Fluffy?"

"Fine," said Tom. "See you then!"

Firefighter Tom carried Fluffy down the hall.

"Spike!" called Tom. "You have company!"

Uh-oh, thought Fluffy. **Who is Spike?**

"Spike" did not sound like a firefighter.

But then, neither did "Fluffy."

Then Fluffy saw Spike.

He was a big white dog with black spots.

He was curled up on his bed.

Spike opened one eye.

Good Spike, thought Fluffy. **Nice doggie**.

Firefighter Tom held Fluffy next to Spike.

Spike sniffed Fluffy.

Fluffy sniffed Spike.

Then Tom put Fluffy down beside Spike.

Spike did not seem to mind.

Neither did Fluffy.

After all, it had been quite a morning.

Fluffy was ready for his afternoon nap.

Maybe he could not be a firefighter.

But he could always dream.

"Wake up, Firefighter Fluffy!"
a voice said.
Fluffy's eyes popped open.
He saw Ms. Day and the whole class.
"We made firefighter posters," said Wade.

Everyone held a poster.

Every poster had a picture of Fluffy on it.

"Good work!" Tom told Ms. Day's class.

"Now Fluffy is a firefighter after all!"

Yes! thought Firefighter Fluffy.
**The best way to fight fires
is to keep them from happening
in the first place!**